THE DENTIST'S PROMISE

MARGARET MAHY

Illustrated by
WENDY SMITH

Hippo

Scholastic Children's Books,
Scholastic Publications Ltd,
7-9 Pratt Street, London NW1 0AE, UK

Scholastic Inc.,
555 Broadway, New York, NY 10012-3999, USA

Scholastic Canada Ltd,
123 Newkirk Road, Richmond Hill,
Ontario, Canada L4C 3G5

Ashton Scholastic Pty Ltd,
PO Box 579, Gosford, New South Wales,
Australia

Ashton Scholastic Ltd,
Private Bag 92801, Penrose, Auckland,
New Zealand

First published in Australia by Omnibus Books, 1991
First published in the UK in hardback by
Scholastic Publications Ltd, 1993
This edition by Scholastic Publications Ltd, 1994

Text copyright © Margaret Mahy, 1991
Illustrations copyright © Wendy Smith, 1991

ISBN: 0 590 55412 3

Typeset by Contour Typesetters, Southall, London
Printed by Cox & Wyman Ltd, Reading, Berks

10 9 8 7 6 5 4 3 2 1

06·95

H J

Oldmouse family tree

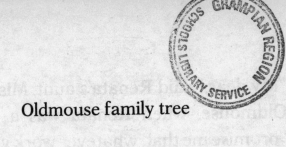
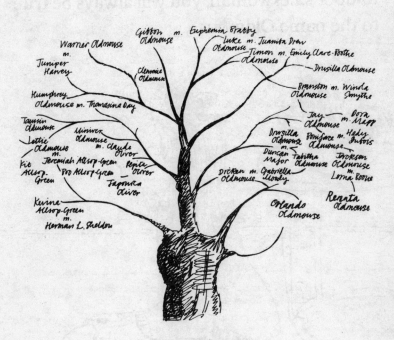

"My dear," said Renata's aunt, Miss Tabitha Oldmouse, when Renata was a little girl, "promise me that, whatever work you decide to do, whether you are a detective or a door-to-door saleswoman, you will always be true to the name Oldmouse.

"There are not many of us left since Great-great-uncle Gibbon Oldmouse fell out of his office window into the middle of a passing circus and was carried off into the unknown. We are an endangered species, so you must stand by that name, Renata, no matter what!"

Renata promised she would always be true to the Oldmouse family name.

She didn't become a door-to-door sales-woman, a dustwoman or a detective. Renata was very fond of smiles, and liked to see them well looked after. She decided to become a dentist.

Miss Tabitha Oldmouse paid for her to be
trained. "But remember your promise!" she
said meaningfully, as she signed a cheque for
her niece's fees.

When Renata went to the College of Dentistry a great many handsome dentists proposed to her, but she turned them all down.

"Never will I give up the name of Oldmouse," she said proudly. "I have promised my aunt that I won't, and an Oldmouse always keeps her promises."

Renata worked hard and was soon awarded her certificate of dentistry.

She bought a tip-back chair, and a drill that played violin music.

"Dentists' rooms don't have to be scary places," she thought, and indeed her surgery was so entertaining that it was hard to get her patients to go home.

People came from far and near because Renata filled teeth so sympathetically.

One day a very good-looking young man came in without an appointment.

"I am sorry to bother you," he said. "I am an acrobat in a travelling circus. My job is swinging by my teeth from a trapeze, and yesterday I chipped one of my teeth. I am told you do very strong repairs. Please help me, if you can." He smiled at Renata.

Renata was fascinated. It would be a joy to repair a smile like his.

"Sit down in my tip-back chair and I'll see what I can do," she promised the young man.

She could see from his expression that he had probably fallen in love with her, and she reminded herself of her promise to her aunt.

"You are the most beautiful dentist I have ever seen," the young man managed to say in a very sincere voice before Renata tipped him backwards so quickly that his breath was taken away.

"Open, please," she said briskly, pretending she hadn't heard, though his words were printed on her thoughts in letters of fire. But when he opened his mouth she couldn't help gasping with delight. Except for one chipped tooth, his teeth were wonderful. There was not a single filling in any of them.

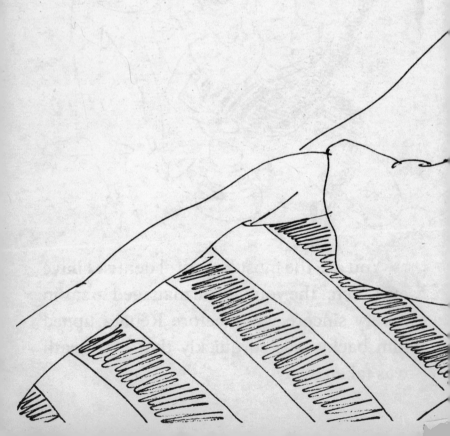

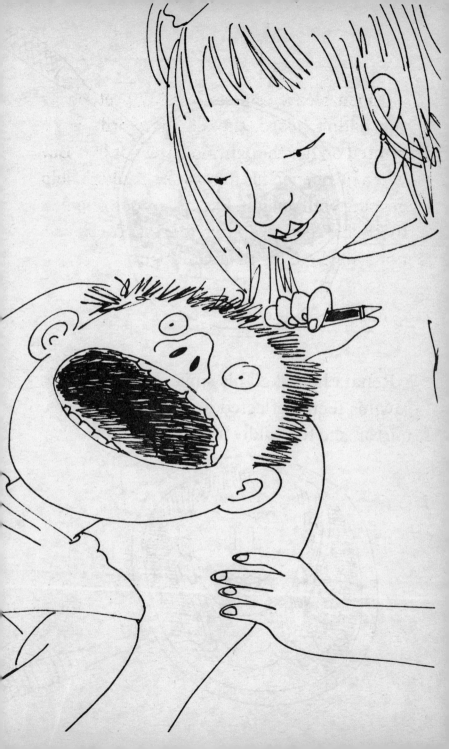

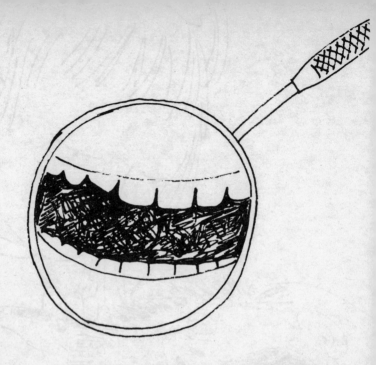

Renata had liked his smile, but when she saw his teeth reflected in her little dentist's mirror, she fell wildly in love with him.

"What beautiful teeth you have," she couldn't help crying.

Of course, the young man could not answer. His mouth was wide open and Renata was gazing into it with her little mirror.

"Aaarrrgh!" he gargled hoarsely.

"I know what you are trying to say," Renata replied, and so she did. Being a dentist had made her very good at working out what people were trying to tell her. "You are asking me to marry you. But it cannot be. You see, I promised my old aunt I would not give up the family name of Oldmouse. All right, rinse, please!"

The young acrobat rinsed his mouth and spat very neatly into the bowl. Then he tried to tell her something, but Renata was too quick for him. She tilted the chair even further back and started to work on the chipped tooth with a little scraping metal thing.

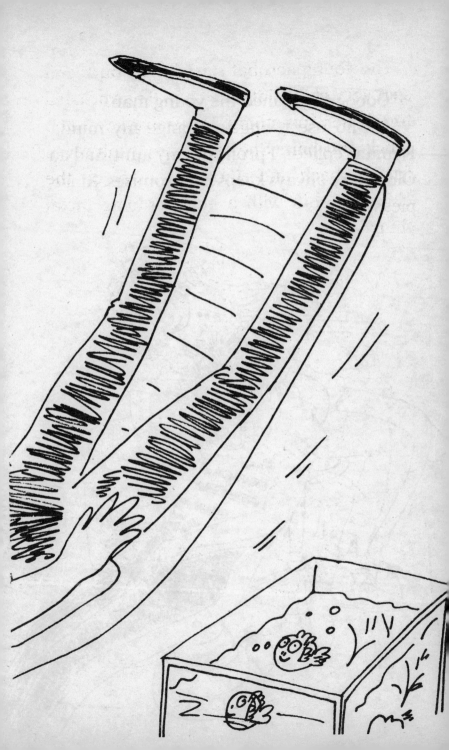

"Ooooer!" groaned the young man.

"It's no use trying to change my mind," Renata replied. "I promised my aunt, and an Oldmouse always keeps her promises. Rinse, please!"

The young man did as he was told. Then he looked at Renata and opened his mouth again. But once more Renata was too quick for him. She was a born dentist.

"I wish things were different," she murmured sadly as she began drilling his tooth in her gentle fashion while violin music filled the air. "I'll tell you honestly—for an Oldmouse is always honest—that there is something about your teeth that has made me fall deeply in love with you."

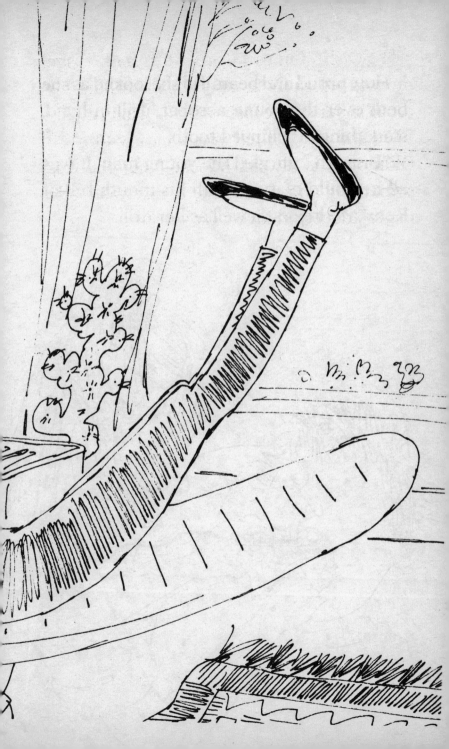

How proud and beautiful she looked as she bent over the young acrobat, drill in hand, smoothing his chipped tooth.

"Urrrrgh," gurgled the young man. It was all he could manage with his mouth full of Renata's fingers as well as her drill.

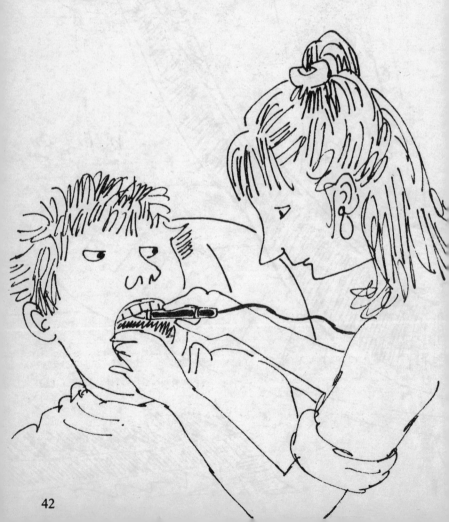

"I know what you are trying to say,"
Renata sighed. "You are begging me to
change my mind. Rinse, please!"

The young man tried to nod his head as he
rinsed, but the special pink rinse went down
the wrong way and he began to choke.

"You must be strong!" cried Renata, patting him on the back with one hand and pushing him down into her dentist's chair with the other.

"You will love again—but someone else,"
she ended with a proud sob.

The acrobat opened his mouth to answer.
Quickly, Renata popped a metal fence around
his chipped tooth and began coating it with a
very strong filling made with special circus
cement.

"You need someone to help you maintain these teeth," she said wistfully. "With me at your side to keep them in perfect condition you could swing by your teeth from a ten-metre pole until you are ninety.

"But my aunt paid for me to go to the College of Dentistry, and I promised her I would be true to the name of Oldmouse. We are an endangered species, you know."

The young man looked lovingly at her as she smoothed off the tooth.

"Now, bite down gently," Renata ordered, taking the metal fence from around his tooth. "There. It is over. I'm afraid there is nothing wrong with the rest of your teeth. Now, we must part." Tears filled her eyes. "Be careful how you bite on that tooth, won't you?" she added, wiping her eyes on a paper towel.

"Dear Miss Oldmouse," the young acrobat replied in rather a funny voice (for half his face was numb), "it is true I fell in love with you at first sight, and felt in my heart that you loved me. But do not despair. We were meant for each other. As it happens, you see,

my name is Oldmouse as well: Orlando Oldmouse, the Ardent Acrobat.

"Marry me! No one will know whether you have my name or I have yours, and we will be Oldmice together."

"Oh, Orlando, let us be married at once, if not sooner," whispered Renata.

Orlando leaped out of the tip-back chair in a single bound and flung his arms around her in an acrobatic embrace.

Then he did seventeen somersaults round and around the tip-back chair all out of sheer happiness, something rarely seen in a dentist's room. Then he and Renata hugged each other again.

No one was more delighted with Orlando than Miss Tabitha Oldmouse. "Why, you must be descended from Great-great-uncle Gibbon Oldmouse," she cried, rushing to print his name on the family tree that took up an entire wall of her small apartment. "Oh, joy! Joy! One more gap filled on the Oldmouse family tree."

"Aunt Tabitha, I plan to marry Orlando," cried Renata boldly.

"Good girl!" Miss Tabitha replied. "I shall be very annoyed if you don't."

Gibbon Oldmouse m.

Warner Oldmouse
m.
Juniper
Harvey

Clemmie
Oldmouse

Humphrey
Oldmouse m. Thomasina Day

Tamsin
Oldmouse

Miniver
Oldmouse
m. Claude
Oliver

Lettie
Oldmouse
m.
Jeremiah Allsop-Green

Pepita
Oliver

Kit
Allsop-
Green

Bob Allsop-Green

Japonica
Oliver

Kevina
Allsop-Green
m.
Herman L. Sheldon

Oldmouse family tree

Euphemia Brabby

Luke m. Juanita Drew
Oldmouse

Timon m. Emily Clare-Boothe
Oldmouse

Drusilla Oldmouse

Branston m. Winola
Oldmouse   Smythe

Jay — Dora
Oldmouse   m. Mapp

Drusilla   Boniface m. Hedy
Oldmouse   Oldmouse   Dubois
m.
Duncan   Tabitha   Jackson
Major   Oldmouse   Oldmouse
m.
Dicken m. Gabriella   Lorna Boone
Oldmouse   Moody

Renata
Oldmouse

Orlando
Oldmouse

61

So Orlando and Renata were married,

and they had several little Oldmice, all of whom had good teeth. They were good acrobats as well, and they all smiled very happily ever after.